BRICKS DOWN

“Chloe imagined falling helplessly, her screams echoing with nobody to hear them and then sinking in icy, murky wetness, never to rise again.

An unpleasant stagnant smell drifted upwards. She pulled herself together and counted the bricks as she passed. ‘One … two … three … ’ When she reached sixteen she shouted, ‘Stop’.”

More great reads in the SHADES 2.0 *series:*

Witness *by Anne Cassidy*
Shouting at the Stars *by David Belbin*
Blitz *by David Orme*
Virus *by Mary Chapman*
Fighting Back *by Helen Orme*
Hunter's Moon *by John Townsend*
Animal Lab *by Malcolm Rose*
Tears of a Friend *by Jo Cotterill*
Danger Money *by Mary Chapman*
A Murder of Crows *by Penny Bates*
Doing the Double *by Alan Durant*
Mantrap *by Tish Farrell*
Coming in to Land *by Dennis Hamley*
Life of the Party *by Gillian Philip*
Plague *by David Orme*
Treachery by Night *by Ann Ruffell*
Mind's Eye *by Gillian Philip*
Gateway from Hell *by David Orme*
Four Degrees More *by Malcolm Rose*
Who Cares? *by Helen Orme*
Cry, Baby *by Jill Atkins*
The Messenger *by John Townsend*
Asteroid *by Malcolm Rose*
Space Explorers *by David Orme*
Hauntings *by Mary Chapman*
The Scream *by Penny Bates*
Rising Tide *by Anne Rooney*
Stone Robbers *by Tish Farrell*
Fire! *by David Orme*
Invasion *by Mary Chapman*
What About Me? *by Helen Orme*
Flood *by David Orme*
The Real Test *by Jill Atkins*
Aftershock *by Jill Atkins*
Mau Mau Brother *by Tish Farrell*
Crying Out *by Clare Lawrence*
Gunshots at Dawn *by Mary Chapman*
The Calling *by Penny Bates*
Ben's Room *by Barbara Catchpole*
The Phoenix Conspiracy *by Mary Chapman*
The Team with the Ghost Player *by Dennis Hamley*
Death on Toast *by John Townsend*
Flashback *by John Townsend*
No Good *by Helen Orme*

SHADES 2.0

Sixteen Bricks Down

Dennis Hamley

SHADES 2.0
Sixteen Bricks Down
by Dennis Hamley

Published by Ransom Publishing Ltd.
Radley House, 8 St. Cross Road, Winchester, Hampshire SO23 9HX, UK
www.ransom.co.uk

ISBN 978 178127 631 0
First published in 2014

A CIP catalogue record of this book is available from the British Library.

CONTENTS

ONE

Not for the first time that day, Chloe wondered what she was doing here.

She chained her bike to a fence by the road and ran over a worn, stone bridge which crossed a dried-up watercourse. She came to a stone gatehouse flanked by two ruined towers. *This is really stupid*, she thought. The July day was hot, but the gatehouse walls struck deathly cold. She leaned against the wall to get her breath back. Then she considered what had happened and what to do now.

Chloe had hated her new stepfather from the moment Mum brought him into the house, two years before.

'Please, love,' Mum pleaded. 'Don't be jealous. We'll get on all right, the three of us, I promise.'

'Why did Dad have to go?' she cried, for the hundredth time.

'It was his choice, love,' said Mum. 'But I can't live on my own.'

Chloe knew better than to say, 'You've got me, haven't you?'

'Well, Jed's moving in,' said Mum firmly. 'Try to get on with him. You'll find he's all right, honestly.'

So Chloe tried. But he wasn't all right. He

didn't like her and let her know it, though not in front of Mum. Still, he didn't seem to like *any* kids – even his own from a partner he'd lived with years ago. Great man.

Jed Gaunt.

Chloe thought the name suited him. A thin name, a name with high cheekbones and a narrow face which always needed a shave. He was lithe, catlike, menacing. She shuddered when he was near her.

An hour earlier, she had been alone in the house, thinking how her dislike of Jed was wrecking her relationship with her mother. Sometimes she thought: *it's him or me.*

The answer came with a dull thud: *it's him.* What then? Run away? Be a missing person? She imagined her tearful mother begging her to return. Jed would add his lying voice to her pleas.

Running away was not an option.

She drifted daringly into their bedroom. A desk stood in one corner. Jed's laptop stood on it, on stand-by. It seemed to say, *his secrets are hidden in here*. Her hand strayed towards the keyboard. She pulled it back, as if it was red hot. Then she decided. *I'll do it.*

A minute later, she was staring at Jed's email inbox.

TWO

The castle seemed deserted. Sometimes archaeologists were there digging things up, but not today.

Once again she wondered – *why am I here? I must be crazy*. She shivered. Perhaps that was because the shade of the gatehouse was cold after the hot sun in the open. Or perhaps …

Someone was watching. She felt it as if

searchlights were focused on her. She turned round slowly.

'Who's there?' she said. She patted the pocket of her jeans. Yes, her phone was there. At least she could call for help.

Footsteps. Someone was crossing the ground beyond the gatehouse. A human figure was framed for a moment in the entrance. A boy, about two years older than she was. His features were indistinct in the shadow of the gatehouse roof. Chloe tried to hide, but she was too late. He had seen her.

'Who are you?' said Chloe. She was suddenly very afraid.

'Steve,' he answered.

'Steve who? What are you doing here?'

'For that matter, what are you?'

'I don't know.' What else could she say?

'Come in the sunlight, where we can see each other,' said Steve.

He walked back into the sunshine. Chloe

hesitantly followed, telling herself that she ought to run away full tilt across the bridge. She noticed a Vespa scooter parked on the other side of the gatehouse, out of the way, so it was pure chance that she had seen it. Once in the sun, she gasped, horrified. *I can't get away from him.*

Steve was thin, with high cheekbones and a narrow face. A young version of her stepfather, except that his face was clear, with no stubble.

'You're his son,' she cried. 'You're waiting for me. He told you!'

'Whose son?' he answered.

'My stepfather's. Jed Gaunt.'

'Rubbish. I don't know anyone called Gaunt.'

'But you look just like him. He *must* be your Dad.'

'I haven't the faintest idea what you're talking about,' said Steve. 'If I don't know him, how can he have told me to wait for you?'

Chloe calmed down. She'd let him speak for

himself.

'Look,' said Steve. 'My surname is Followes. My father is Mr Followes and my mother is Mrs Followes. Any more questions?'

Though Steve might look like Jed, his face had no menace in it. He had a nice smile.

'I'm sorry,' she said. 'It's such a coincidence. You're the living image of my stepfather. I thought you must be his son.'

'I see,' said Steve. 'Well, I'm not, so don't worry.' He looked at her shrewdly. 'You don't like your stepfather, do you?'

'No I don't,' Chloe replied.

'I'm sorry about that,' said Steve. 'Still, we can't like everybody.'

Chloe still wanted to run away. But this boy looked as though he'd catch her without raising a sweat.

'So what are you doing here?' said Steve. Then, still shrewdly, 'Is it something to do with your stepfather? You seem to have him on the brain.'

'Yes,' said Chloe, and regretted it at once.

'Well what is it?'

She wanted to say, 'That's my business; nothing to do with you.' But she dearly wanted someone to tell her she wasn't being stupid. She blurted out, 'I opened his laptop and looked at his email. I shouldn't have, but I did.'

'So?'

'I read his latest email.'

'Naughty,' said Steve. 'Did you get more than you bargained for?'

She'd told him too much. In her mind she saw the message as clearly as it came up on the screen. Thinking about what she'd done made her shudder.

The title of the unread message was:

RE: next step.

Chloe clicked on it.

Jed. I saw Mo when I was inside and he told

me a lot. The doings from the VMAG job are well hidden until the heat's off and they can be collected safely.

Mo doesn't know who did the job cos he wasn't in on that bit of the scam. Mr Fattorini keeps his plans to himself. But Mo says it's to do with some castle and something about sixteen bricks down. Does Rokeby Castle ring a bell?

Don't let Fattorini find out about this or you'll end up six feet under Epping Forest. So might he if anything goes wrong. Russian oligarchs don't mess around.

Delete this.

Dave

Certain words jumped out at her. *When I was inside*. Dave and Mo must have been in prison. Might Jed have met them there? That would be something her mother didn't know.

Who was Mr Fattorini? What did Russian oligarchs have to do with it? There was something from, well, it sounded like a robbery, hidden in – *Rokeby Castle?* That was only three miles away, deserted and desolate, none of the smooth grass of a National Trust site.

What did *sixteen bricks down* mean? Or *six feet under Epping Forest?* Well, she got that one. Horrible. Not even for Jed would she want that. Daringly, she pressed *Print*. The printer clacked, she tore the paper out and stuffed it in a pocket of her jeans.

Then she heard footsteps coming up the stairs and knew whose they were at once. Had he heard the printer? Hastily she closed the email and crept out.

Too late. Jed saw her on the stairs. His face twisted into pure malevolence.

'If I thought you'd been in that bedroom and meddled with anything of mine, I'd kill you,' he said. 'I'm not joking, Chloe. Don't bother telling your mother, because she won't believe you.'

So he hadn't heard the printer. 'I haven't been in there,' she gasped. 'Honest.'

'You'd better not have.' He stalked into the bedroom and slammed the door behind him.

She stole softly downstairs into the kitchen. Three minutes later, Jed ran downstairs, through the front door to his car. She rushed to a front window to watch him.

Before he opened the door, he made a call on his mobile. Then he got in and she saw him turn left onto the road. Rokeby Castle was the other way. She looked at her watch. Half-past two.

It was then that the mad idea came. *I'll go to Rokeby Castle and see if I can find what he means by sixteen bricks down.*

So she took her bike and set off.

'Well, did you?' Steve asked again.

'Did I what?'

'Get more than you bargained for?'

Chloe's mind was full of questions. *Do I trust him? I don't know what I'm looking for. If he helped me, we might work it out together.*

She made up her mind.

She pulled the scrumpled email printout from her pocket and handed it to him. Frowning, he read it and said, 'I'm not surprised you don't like him.'

'I thought that once I was here, I'd know what *sixteen bricks down* meant.'

'You mean you want to find this thing from the job this Dave is talking about? Are you sure about that? He'd kill you. Anyway, what does VMAG stand for?'

'I don't know. Should I tell the police?'

Steve didn't answer. He looked at the huge keep in the middle of the castle grounds. 'I wouldn't say this place is built with bricks. Bits of rock more like.'

The walls were made of flint and covered in

straggly ivy.

'Sixteen bricks down,' Steve murmured. 'What could be made of bricks here? If it was a wall, wouldn't he say "sixteen bricks up"?'

'Could it be a hole in the ground?' said Chloe.

'A hole in the ground lined with bricks?' said Steve. 'What could that be?'

They looked at each other and exclaimed together: 'A well!'

'It's worth trying,' said Steve.

THREE

Chloe knew that even though he'd driven off in the opposite direction, Jed could have picked a mate up and still got to the castle before she did. His car wasn't there, but she kept listening in case he turned up after all.

Steve's uncanny resemblance still worried her, though she couldn't help both liking and believing him.

They tramped over the rough ground, but saw nothing remotely like a well.

'This is no good,' said Steve. 'Let's think.'

'Wouldn't a well be at the lowest point, so the water would be easier to bring up?' said Chloe.

'Probably,' said Steve. He looked round. 'What's that?'

A huge, ruined building. The roof was open to the sky.

'The keep,' said Chloe.

'Let's see,' replied Steve. They entered through where there must once have been a huge door. Inside, they were surrounded by the massive, high circular wall. The ground was pitted and irregular.

It was hard to imagine medieval lords, ladies and knights banqueting with scullions and kitchen maids scurrying round to serve them. In one corner was a sudden dip, as if there had once been steps down to a lower level.

'Perhaps the kitchens were here,' said Chloe. It could be a likely place for a well.'

But there was no well. Chloe picked her way carefully, saw nothing and was about to give up, when Steve called out from the other side of the keep.

'Over here.'

She joined him where worn stone steps led down and disappeared into a dark hole, like an entrance to a cave.

'Those steps look safe,' said Steve. 'Shall we?'

Chloe bit down sudden fear. 'Yes,' she said firmly.

Together they stepped gingerly downwards. The stairway turned in a spiral. They could walk side by side, each with one hand tracing the walls encircling them.

Chloe caught Steve's free hand. At the foot of the stairway they came out into unexpected light. Chloe looked up. She saw clear sky.

'This place once had a roof,' she said. The floor was firm and level, and in the centre was ...

'A well,' Chloe breathed in wonderment, as if she had won the lottery. 'We guessed right.'

'It must have been here for seven hundred years,' said Steve.

Round the mouth of the well was a parapet about half a metre high, made not of flint but brick.

'Why brick?' said Steve. 'Why not flint like everything else here?'

'It might have been made later,' said Chloe.

'Or rebuilt,' said Steve.

Chloe got down on hands and knees and looked over the parapet into inky darkness. Steve dropped a stone in. They heard a tiny splash a very long time afterwards.

'The doings from the VMAG job must be down there,' said Steve.

Across the well was a drum coiled with rope

and a huge handle.

'This isn't seven hundred years old,' said Steve. 'The rope's hardly worn.'

The rope was tied to a huge steel bucket, big enough to hold gallons of water and even a full-grown human being.

'That's not medieval, either,' said Chloe. 'Someone's been here.'

'Jackpot,' said Steve. 'An old well which someone's just been to. This is the place.'

'Now what do we do?' said Chloe.

'I'll get in the bucket,' said Steve. 'You winch me down slowly and I'll count sixteen bricks down. Then stop turning and wait while I look.'

'No.' Chloe was firm. 'I go in the bucket. I'm lighter than you and you'll be stronger than me. So you hold the rope. Besides, I wouldn't wind you down slowly enough, let alone stand your weight.'

'You don't have to,' said Steve. 'There are

catches here, so you can stop the handle when I tell you and lock it in place.'

'I'd still have to lower you. I'm going in the bucket.'

Steve thought for a moment and then said, 'I've tried to be a gentleman but, yes, you're right. Get in.'

He pulled the rope to the side, so she could stand on the parapet and step in the bucket. It swayed dangerously and the rope creaked. She swallowed down her fright and gasped, 'Lower it now.'

Steve strained on the handle. At first the bucket hardly moved: then it dropped slowly and evenly. Chloe thought of the long wait before the stone Steve threw had reached the water. She imagined following it, falling helplessly, her screams echoing with nobody to hear them and then sinking in icy, murky wetness, never to rise again.

She would have nightmares about this. An

unpleasant stagnant smell drifted upwards. She pulled herself together and counted the courses of bricks as she passed.

'One … two … three … '

When she reached sixteen she shouted, 'Stop'. She felt a sudden firmness as the catch took the weight.

'Can you see?' Steve called.

'Not very well,' she answered. 'Pull the rope over to the side so the bucket comes closer to the bricks.'

The bucket swayed again, until she was close enough to touch them. She marked out the sixteenth course and felt round three above and three below to be on the safe side. The bricks were old and the mortar was crumbling.

'Pull the rope round the side of the well, so I can get further round,' she shouted.

The bucket swayed again. Nothing – no sign of any tampering.

'Round again,' she called.

Nothing.

'And again.'

This time there was something. A square of newer bricks, four bricks wide, six down. They looked newly repointed.

'I think I've found the place,' she called up. 'I need something to chip the cement away. Like a chisel and mallet.'

'Fat chance,' Steve replied. A moment's silence, then: 'I know. Flints. If they were good enough for Stone Age man, they're good enough for us. Wait there.'

'I'm not going anywhere,' she called, but he was gone.

She felt very alone and fearful. Only a thin sheet of metal and a rope kept her from that dreadful plummeting fall. It seemed an age before a voice said, 'Got them.'

'Winch me up and give them to me,' she answered.

She felt the catch being removed, a sudden scary lightness, then the bucket moved steadily upward. But before the bucket reached the top it stopped suddenly.

'Carry on turning,' she cried.

'No need,' was the answer. 'I'll just drop them to you.'

She felt the bucket pulled over to the side again. She couldn't see Steve's face as he leaned over, but she could make out the thin shoulders.

'I've found two which look OK. I'm dropping them now. Make sure you get them. One.'

A large, pointed flint dropped in the bucket with a metallic clatter.

'Two.'

Another.

'Keep the bucket pulled over,' she shouted, as he lowered it again.

She jabbed a flint at the cement. It merely jarred her hand and left no mark. She'd have to use one flint as a mallet and the pointed end of the other as a chisel.

At first, all she did was turn the cement into powder. But she patiently chipped away until she made real inroads. One brick was almost free. Perhaps if she pulled at it ...

It wouldn't move. She attacked the remaining pointing, then pulled again. Gradually the brick became free.

'Done it!' she shouted. She reached through the hole it had left.

Thin air.

But, she reasoned, if there was nothing behind this brick, then she'd have to knock more out. She jabbed the sharp end of one flint into the cement and hammered it hard with the other. After a few minutes she turned her attention to the bricks themselves.

And soon, satisfyingly, she knocked out first one, then another. They plopped inwards into the hole and she heard them land on something solid a foot or so below. She stopped to think what this might mean. Could there be a whole chamber gouged out of the well and covered over with bricks?

She attacked the other bricks. One by one they fell backwards into the chamber. Soon she had opened an aperture about forty centimetres square. She leaned out of the bucket as far as she dared and groped round inside the chamber.

At first, she only felt bricks. Then her fingers touched something different. She got a firm hold on it and pulled it out. A scroll made of canvas.

'I've found it,' she called.

'How many?'

'Only one.'

'Look again.'

So she reached out again, scrabbled round and found five similar canvas rolls.

'Six,' she shouted up. 'Two are quite small.

The others are much bigger.'

'All right. I'll pull you up now.'

She felt the bucket rise and heard the rope creak. Above her she saw Steve's thin silhouette.

Halfway up, she had a thought which made her stomach turn: *what made him think there was more than one? There's something wrong.*

Suddenly, a glaring light blinded her. A powerful torch shone into her eyes. But Steve hadn't got a torch.

The bucket stopped with her head level with the top of the parapet.

'You can hand them over now, Chloe,' said a voice.

It wasn't Steve's. It was Jed's.

FOUR

'Where's Steve?' she cried.

'Never mind Steve. Hand them over.'

She stubbornly held onto the canvas rolls. Jed lowered the torch. His face was still in shadow, but she saw that he held a knife against the rope.

'Hand them over,' he said. 'Or I cut the rope.'

She didn't move.

'Don't think I wouldn't,' said Jed. His voice chilled her heart. 'You'd never be found and I'd be rid of a nuisance. Your mother would soon forget you, now she has me.'

'No she wouldn't,' Chloe cried.

Jed laughed. 'Wouldn't she now? You'd be surprised.'

Dumbly, she handed the rolls up to him.

'Clever girl,' he said. 'Even so, I think I'll let you stew a bit.' He lowered the bucket slowly down again, until it was two metres below where it was before.

'You can wait there until I'm back. Might be an hour, might be all night for all I know. Perhaps I'll let you back up. Though perhaps I won't. You know too much.'

The torch was switched off. She was left in cold darkness, swinging helplessly in a bucket suspended over stagnant water far below. She curled up on the floor of the bucket and cried.

She had no idea how long she stayed there with her eyes closed. But she opened them to a faint, cold light. Had she slept? Was it night time? She looked up. A bright moon shone overhead. Of course: she'd forgotten the well was open to the sky.

She had a wild idea. Did she dare try climbing up the side using the pointing between the bricks as footholds? The very thought made her shudder. Even so, she looked hard at the shaft's walls.

And she saw something. An iron rung set in the wall, level with the rim of the bucket. She looked further up. Yes: another, and above that, five more. She sat back to take this in. She'd found a ladder to the top of the shaft, set in the wall.

But it was out of reach.

Perhaps she could make the bucket sway nearer. She pushed as if she was sitting on a swing. At first the bucket hardly moved. Then it gained momentum. But it wouldn't keep straight because it was held by one rope, not two.

By the time she had the knack of making it swing towards the rim, she was worn out. But she came close enough to catch the iron rung, hold it and stop the bucket from swinging back to the middle. The rung was safe and firm, with no rust.

It must have been put there recently, too. Perhaps Jed did it. If one rung was strong, surely the others would be.

She stayed clinging to the rung for a long time before she dared move. In the end she forced herself.

Once she hoisted herself out of the bucket to climb the iron ladder, the bucket would swing back. Then there would be nothing between her and an unimaginable drop into boundless, permanent darkness.

But if she stayed where she was, then when Jed came back he might cut the rope. She knew in her heart that he would slice it through without a second thought.

She took a deep breath and braced herself. She strained upwards until her right foot was on the lowest rung. Then she reached up to the rung above, hoisted her left foot out of the bucket, grabbed the next rung and felt the bucket swing away to hit the side of the well with a clanging thud.

There was no going back now.

She hugged the wall and for a moment couldn't move for sheer panic. Her fingers were weakening. She was losing her grip, she was about to plummet down …

She willed herself to reach for the next rung and painfully hoisted her right leg to the rung below. Five rungs to go. She felt cautiously confident now and tried to gather speed. But her left foot slipped off the next rung.

She nearly let go with the shock, her heart beat wildly, and she had to cling to the side to collect her wits.

Stay slow, stay slow.

Next rung – reach with hand, grip, hoist, make foot firm. All the while she looked up towards the moon.

At last, she reached the parapet. She scrambled over it, fell on the hard ground and wept with relief. The climb seemed to have taken half her lifetime.

Then she dried her eyes and considered her situation. Steve. He'd known all along what would happen. He was Jed's son, whatever he said.

To think she'd been taken in so easily. He'd never said why he was here and once they were on the hunt for the well she forgot to make him.

Two-faced treachery which nearly ended in her death, that's what it was. She hated him with every fibre of her being.

But hating Steve wouldn't help her now. She had to get out of here.

She picked her way up the steps, out of the keep, ghostly and forbidding in the moonlight, through the gatehouse, and over the bridge to the road.

FIVE

She noticed that the scooter was still there. Did that mean that Steve was still here too? As she expected, her bike was gone. Now what was she to do?

As she stood undecided, the road to her left was lit up by headlights. *I can get a lift*, she thought joyfully. But a warning voice told her to hide in the ditch by the road.

The lights belonged to a covered lorry, with HARBEN'S PIANOS painted on the side in gold letters. It stopped with its rear doors opposite where Chloe hid. The door on the passenger side opened.

'I'll sort her out now. There'll be no trace. Back in three minutes.'

Jed's voice. He jumped out and ran towards the gatehouse. So he was going to get rid of her.

She crouched trembling in the ditch. Soon Jed came back, opened the van door and swung himself in.

'Done it,' she heard him say. That meant he must have cut the rope, but hadn't noticed she wasn't in the bucket.

She nearly fainted with the horror of her narrow escape. Then she realised he thought she was out of the way for good. That meant she had an advantage over him. The thought almost made her laugh.

The lorry slowly began to move. She noticed

a platform at the back. Some sort of electric lift. A mad idea came to her. She dashed out from the ditch, jumped, landed on the platform and grabbed the handle of the rear door before the lorry could gather speed.

Soon the lorry was bucketing along quite fast: Chloe braced herself firmly on the platform, hung on to the handle and watched the road rush by underneath her.

They twisted and turned down minor roads and narrow lanes. She had no idea where they were until they passed through a tiny village. By the light of the dim street lamps, Chloe could see the time on her watch. 11.30. Mum would be frantic by now.

As they left the village, she saw a receding notice: THANK YOU FOR DRIVING CAREFULLY THROUGH LOWER CLAYSTONE. She knew Lower Claystone. It was ten miles west of her own town.

The lorry turned sharply right, into what

looked like a small, rundown industrial estate, bumped over a potholed yard and stopped outside an unlit building. Chloe read the sign: HARBEN'S PIANO WAREHOUSE.

Now what? She couldn't stay on this platform. She had to be gone before they got out of the van. She jumped off and hid round the wall of the warehouse. Peering round the corner, she saw Jed and the driver get out.

They came to the rear of the lorry and opened the door. Jed reached in, pulled out her bike, hurled it to the ground and said, 'We'll lose that later. She won't need it any more.' Then they sauntered to the front of the building and went inside.

Daringly she ran forward and seized her bike. She nearly jumped on and pedalled away. But they'd see it was gone and probably catch her long before she got home. No. She must find out what was going on.

A light was switched on inside the

warehouse. She crept to the door and tried the handle. It was not locked. She eased it silently open into a wide, high-ceilinged hall full of highly polished grand pianos. In one wall were three doors. She tiptoed past them, listening.

Voices sounded from behind the middle door. She stopped. She didn't recognise the first voice.

'What about the boy?'

'You needn't worry about him.'

Jed's voice.

'He knows which side his bread's buttered on.'

The first voice said, 'If you say so. We'll stuff the loot into the new Steinway and deliver it tomorrow. That'll be a cool two hundred grand each. As long as Fattorini doesn't twig. If he does, we're dead.'

'He won't,' said Jed. 'He'll go after Mo and Dave. He won't find us. You can be sure Dave deleted the email he sent me. I know I did.

That girl read it, but we won't be hearing from her again. Trust me.'

'I hope you're right.'

The door opened. Chloe jumped behind the nearest piano, a large grand. They didn't see her as they passed. She stole from piano to piano as they strode past them, until she came to the other side of the warehouse. They still hadn't come to the Steinway they wanted and she had run out of pianos.

But there was another door open in front of her. She scurried across to it like a soldier in no-man's-land and into the room behind. If she held the door slightly open she could still watch them from here.

Jed's companion lifted the lid of a grand piano with STEINWAY written in gold letters over the keyboard. He carefully placed the six scrolls inside and replaced the lid. But instead of going back the way they had come, they walked straight towards her door. Desperately she eased it shut. There was a bolt on the inside and she pushed it across.

'What was that noise?' she heard Jed say sharply.

'Rats,' said the other, 'The place is full of them.'

She waited for them to leave, but their voices droned on as if they were going to stay there all night. A little moonlight through a tiny window told her where she was. Her heart sank. She had locked herself in the loo.

The pedestal was white, with a black plastic lid and cover and a cistern high up with a pull-chain to flush it. She really wanted to use it, but she daren't. Being trapped here wasn't as bad as the well, but could be just as dangerous. What if they wanted to go to the loo, too?

If they found the door locked, they'd break it down. They'd haul her out and her great escape would go for nothing. She stood on the lavatory lid and reached up to the little window over the pedestal. She wrenched the rusted catch open and leaned out.

It was hardly two metres to the ground, but the window was so small she'd never squeeze through, especially with the cistern in the way. But what else could she do?

Perhaps she could draw her knees up and force herself out. But she might lose her balance and fall on her head. That would not be good.

She grasped the window frame and tried it. Useless. She was stuck. Getting out of the well was child's play compared to this.

She tried to wriggle back in, but was stuck that way as well.

A thin figure was approaching from outside. Panic: it was Jed, and this time he would make no mistake.

SIX

The thin figure came close. Chloe went cold with fear. She'd escaped him once, but she wouldn't escape him again.

Then the moonlight lit up his face. It wasn't Jed, it was Steve. She went cold again. If anything, this might be worse.

'Chloe, what are you doing here?' he whispered. 'Jed said he'd taken care of you. I didn't like to think what he meant.'

'Go away, you rat. You're worse than he is. I'd rather stay stuck than be helped by you.'

'It's not what you think. You can't stay there. You'll have to let me help you.'

'Go *away*. I can look after myself.'

'Look, I'm on your side. Trust me.'

'How can I any more?'

'You'll have to. I'm the only chance you've got.'

She couldn't see an alternative. She had to believe him. 'All right,' she muttered.

'Reach down,' said Steve. He took hold of her wrists and pulled.

'You're pulling my arms out of my sockets,' she cried.

'*Push*,' he hissed. 'And don't make so much noise.'

She felt herself move forward a little, though her hips were being skinned alive. Something lumpy dug into her skin.

'Harder,' said Steve, as he pulled. The lumpy thing was now really hurting her.

Centimetre by centimetre she emerged, until she was free and saw the ground close below. Steve steadied her until she was standing safe on the ground, hurting all over.

'Right,' said Steve. 'I've got to explain. I wasn't quite straight with you. Yes, I am Jed's son. I'm sorry I misled you, but I wasn't telling lies about my parents. The Followes family adopted me. I took their surname and for a long time thought I was their real son.

'Two years ago Jed turned up and put pressure on me. Said he could take me back because he was my real father and could prove it. And he would, unless I did what he said and told nobody. I believed him.

'I didn't know that, as I was legally adopted, he couldn't touch me. It didn't take long to see he was a crook. I knew that one day he'd find a way to make me help him. But I was too scared to tell anybody.'

'And did he find a way?' asked Chloe.

'Not till today. He rang me this afternoon on my mobile. How did he get my number? That's scary.'

'They can do anything now,' said Chloe. 'What time was this?'

'About half-past two.'

'I saw him make the call,' she said.

'He said if I met him at Rokeby Castle by three, I'd end up much richer and never hear from him again. I went because I had some crazy idea that if I knew what he was doing, I could go to the police. So I got on my scooter and came as quick as I could. So fast that I forgot to bring my mobile. When I saw you there, I daren't tell you the truth. My life of crime might have begun today. But we found out what he's up to together.'

'But I still don't know what he's up to! He hid the scrolls in the piano. What are they?'

'I think I may have sussed that out. Do you remember a big art theft a year ago?'

'No. Why should I?'

'Well, I do. I remember my art teacher going on about it. She was really upset.'

'Why?'

'Because some really great paintings disappeared. Worth millions. The thieves knew what they were doing. They broke into the gallery, took the canvases out of the frames and even put prints in their place, so people wouldn't notice at once.'

'Why are they so valuable?'

'They were stolen from the VMAG. That's the Victorian Masters Art Gallery in London. A Turner, a Millais, a Holman Hunt, a Whistler and two Dante Gabriel Rossettis. Really famous painters. The paintings are worth five million at least.'

'What's that got to do with Jed?'

'Well, I think these scrolls are those

paintings. Jed didn't steal them, but he knew who did. This man called Dave found out from someone he met in prison.'

'Mo,' said Chloe. 'He was mentioned in Dave's email.'

'Jed worked out where the scrolls were. He was furious when he found you with me. I told him you'd turned up out of the blue and shown me the email. I thought that if we tried to look for the paintings, we'd have them ready for him and he'd be pleased. Well, that's nearly true.'

'And he believed you?' said Chloe.

'He must have thought, *like father, like son*.'

'Who's Fattorini?'

'Ah, yes. I think this is what happened. Someone stole the paintings for Luigi Fattorini, who's a London art dealer. Bit of a crook, too. I think he had some rich private buyer lined up.'

'What would Jed do with them?' said Chloe.

‘Fattorini would kill him if he found out he’d got them.’

‘Perhaps he’d deserve it,’ said Steve. ‘Jed’s in with another crook, Harben, who runs this piano warehouse. If they could find the paintings for another foreign buyer, he’ll pay them far more than they’d get from Fattorini. It’s worth the risk.’

‘The Russian oligarch,’ said Chloe. ‘He’s the foreign buyer. They’ve hidden the paintings in a Steinway grand piano and now they’re taking them somewhere. The next stage on their journey to the oligarch.’

‘How did you know that?’ Steve exclaimed.

‘I wasn’t trapped in the loo for fun,’ Chloe answered.

‘Well, what can we do?’ said Steve.

‘I don’t know,’ Chloe replied. Then the pain in her body eased enough for her to realise what the lump was that dug into her as she struggled through the window. ‘My phone,’ she breathed. 'I forgot I had it. I could have saved us all this.'

'Quick,' said Steve. '999.'

She dialled and gasped, 'Police. Harben's piano ware ... '

Suddenly a hard hand was clamped over her mouth and the phone seized out of her hand.

'Oh no you don't,' said Jed.

SEVEN

Chloe struggled hopelessly as Jed threw her phone away into the darkness. She heard the crunch as it smashed on a brick wall. Steve was pinioned as well.

'What shall we do with this pair then, Jed?' said the man who had seized him.

'I'll take her back to where she's supposed to be already,' Jed replied grimly. 'She got out once, but she won't do it again. He can go down there with her.'

'But I'm your son,' Steve cried.

'So what?' said Jed. 'Throw them in the van, Harben, and let's get driving.'

'What about the bike?'

'It goes down the well with them. Shove it in the back.'

Harben opened the rear doors of the van and they were pushed in. The doors were slammed and they heard the lock clunk. They were in pitch darkness.

'Traps,' said Chloe. 'My third trap of the day.'

'Third time lucky,' said Steve. 'Let's hope.'

'My bike must be somewhere in this van,' said Chloe. A moment later, 'There's something else in here as well. I'm nearly stuck in the corner.'

'Let me get over there and have a look,' said Steve. A moment later he said, 'It's a grand piano.'

'It's the Steinway with the paintings hidden inside,' said Chloe.

'Yes!' cried Steve, triumphantly but softly.

'If we could get out of here we could take the paintings with us on the bike.'

'You can try if you like,' said Steve. 'The rear doors are locked and we're doing fifty miles an hour.'

Silence. Then Chloe said, 'Could we use the piano as a sort of battering ram?'

'We'll try anything,' said Steve.

'We must take the paintings out first,' said Chloe.

'We'll pluck at the strings. Any strings sounding muffled could have the scrolls wedged under them,' said Steve.

So they leaned over the piano's frame and plucked each string in turn, Chloe from the top, Steve from the bass notes. Round about the middle the strings didn't sound a clear note but a muffled 'clunk'.

'Here they are,' said Steve. Two scrolls were wedged underneath the strings. Gently they took them out.

'These are the small ones. I can stuff one down my top,' said Chloe.

'Two's enough,' said Steve. 'Mine goes inside my shirt. We'll soon be at the castle. Let's move this thing.'

Finding places to wedge into so they could push was difficult in the dark. At last Chloe said, 'I've got a grip here,' and Steve answered, 'Me too. One, two, three, *push*.'

The piano hardly moved. 'Again,' he cried. '*Push*.'

Three more pushes made the piano move until it gently touched the door. 'Again,' said Steve. 'Its weight might be enough to break the lock.'

Another push and then a loud snap. 'Amazing. We've broken it!' Steve exclaimed happily. He pushed at the door and it swung open, letting a blast of cold air in.

The road winding away behind them was an alarming sight, lit up by the headlights of a following car. They waved desperately to catch the driver's attention.

'We'd kill ourselves if we tried to jump,' said Chloe. 'Wait until the van slows.'

'That might be too late,' said Steve.

But the van braked violently and slowed almost to a stop.

'*Now*,' shouted Steve. 'Aim for the verge.'

He hurled Chloe's bike out, took her hand and they jumped together to fall bruisingly on grass, as the van picked up speed and skidded round the sharp bend which had made Harben brake so suddenly.

'I told you third time lucky,' Steve gasped. The car following also braked violently and stopped. A furious driver jumped out.

'What in God's name does that maniac think he's doing?' he shouted. 'He nearly killed us all. Don't worry, I've got his number.'

'Can you ring the police?' said Chloe. 'I would, but I've lost my mobile. Tell them the Harben's piano van is just coming up to Rokeby Castle and it's got four stolen paintings hidden in the Steinway. We've got the other two.'

'Are you having me on?' said the man.

'No,' said Steve. 'Do it. Please.'

'OK, I'll believe you,' said the driver. He gave the message exactly as Chloe had said, adding the van's registration number.

'Now could you ring my mum to tell her I'm all right?' she asked. 'This is the number … '

'Can I give you two a lift?' he asked when he had finished. 'You can put that wreck of a bike in the boot.'

They sat together in the back seat, clutching the scrolls, relaxing in the car's warmth and listening to a CD playing softly. But, after hardly a mile the driver shouted,

'Oh, not them again,' and drew to a halt. The van was in the ditch, lit up by cars with flashing blue lights.

In the glare, they saw two dark figures making for the hedge at the side of the road, with more figures chasing them.

'Police,' said the driver. 'They've got them.'

'There's more behind us,' said Chloe. Two more police cars stopped behind them, blue lights flashing. A policeman got out of the first.

'Which of you made the 999 call from the warehouse?' he shouted.

'I did,' Chloe answered.

'Who was the man we heard threaten you?'

'You're chasing him,' said Steve. 'He's my father, but I don't want to know him.' He pulled out the scroll stuffed down his shirt.

'You'll be wanting this,' he said. 'Chloe's got one as well. The other four are bigger. You'll find them in the grand piano.'

'It's a long story,' said Chloe. Then, 'He tried to kill me.'

'If you find the rope cut over the old well at Rokeby Castle, you'll know she's telling the truth,' said Steve.

'Don't worry, we'll look,' said the policeman. 'The van was spotted going like the clappers through Lower Claystone. Harben's Pianos. We've been watching that place for some time now. We put two and two together and tried a pincer movement on them. When we heard the second call we knew we'd got them.'

'Look,' said Chloe.

Jed and Harben were being led handcuffed towards the police cars facing the van. 'Jed's gone, and he won't come back. Mum and I are free, though she might not see it like that to start with.'

'I reckon they'll be in for a good long stretch,' said the policeman. 'Especially if we can do him for attempted murder as well.

We'll get all three of you to the station so you can make a statement.'

'What about your scooter, Steve?' said Chloe. 'It's still at the castle.'

'We'll find it,' said the policeman.

Chloe turned to Steve.

'I suppose we won't see each other again. Till there's a court case,' she said.

'Oh, but we will,' said Steve. 'Very soon. As long as you can forgive me for being my father's son.'

'Of course I can,' Chloe replied and took his hand. 'But this will be a big shock for Mum. She'll just have to get over it. She'll have to buy me a new phone. And a bike.'